Tell Me Why

WHY?

I Talk In My Sleep

Fitchburg Public Library
5530 Lacy Road
Fitchburg, WI 53711
WITHDRAWN

Samantha Bell

Published in the United States of America by Cherry Lake Publishing
Ann Arbor, Michigan
www.cherrylakepublishing.com

Content Adviser: Charisse Gencyuz, M.D., Clinical Instructor, Department of Internal Medicine, University of Michigan
Reading Adviser: Marla Conn, ReadAbility, Inc.

Photo Credits: © bonzodog/Shutterstock Images, cover, 1, 7; © Samuel Borges Photography/Shutterstock Images, cover, 1, 17; © rmnoa357/Shutterstock Images, cover, 1, 21; © Mat Hayward/Shutterstock Images, cover, 1, 15; © Zurijeta/Shutterstock Images, cover, 1, 11; © Nomad_Soul/Shutterstock Images, cover, 1; © michaeljung/Shutterstock Images, back cover; © CREATISTA/Shutterstock Images, 5; © Blend Images/Shutterstock Images, 7; © mattomedia Werbeagentur/Shutterstock Images, 9; © Tom Wang/Shutterstock Images, 13; © Aletia/Shutterstock Images, 17; © Rob Marmion/Shutterstock Images, 19; © YURALAITS ALBERT/Shutterstock Images, 21

Copyright ©2015 by Cherry Lake Publishing
All rights reserved. No part of this book may be reproduced or utilized in any form or by any means without written permission from the publisher.

Library of Congress Cataloging-in-Publication Data

Bell, Samantha, author.
 I talk in my sleep / by Samantha Bell.
     pages cm. -- (Tell me why)
 Summary: "Offers answers to the most compelling questions about sleep talking. Age-appropriate explanations and appealing photos. Additional text features and search tools, including a glossary and an index, help students locate information and learn new words."-- Provided by publisher
 Audience: K to grade 3.
 Includes bibliographical references and index.
 ISBN 978-1-63188-005-6 (hardcover) -- ISBN 978-1-63188-048-3 (pbk.) -- ISBN 978-1-63188-091-9 (pdf) -- ISBN 978-1-63188-134-3 (ebook) 1. Sleeptalking--Juvenile literature. 2. Sleep disorders--Juvenile literature. I. Title.
RC547.B454 2015
154.6--dc23
                                2014005672

Cherry Lake Publishing would like to acknowledge the work of The Partnership for 21st Century Skills. Please visit *www.p21.org* for more information.

Printed in the United States of America
Corporate Graphics Inc.

Table of Contents

Don't Remember That? 4

Sleep Stages 8

Keeping Others Awake 12

Routines Can Help 18

Think About It 22

Glossary 23

Find Out More 23

Index 24

About the Author 24

Don't Remember That?

Penny loved sleepovers. She was excited when her friend Ann came to spend the night.

The girls had a lot of fun together. Then they finally went to sleep. But someone woke Penny up. She looked at Ann. Ann was talking.

"Yes," Ann said. "Let's go. I want that. No fun." Then Ann was quiet again.

Penny did not know what Ann was talking about. And Ann was not awake. She was talking in her sleep.

You may have heard a friend sleep talking during a sleepover.

Lots of people talk in their sleep. Doctors call it **somniloquy**. Sometimes the words make sense. Sometimes they are jumbled. Sleep talkers can whisper, mumble, or shout. They might look like they are talking to someone in their dreams. Whatever they do, they will not remember it. They won't even wake themselves up doing it.

Sleep talkers sometimes wake up other people, like Ann woke up Penny. But what makes people talk in their sleep?

ASK QUESTIONS!

Has anyone ever heard you talk in your sleep? Ask your parents, siblings, or friends. Could they understand what you were saying?

Sometimes sleep talkers are loud enough to wake others.

Sleep Stages

Sometimes when people talk in their sleep, other people listen in. They hope the sleep talker will tell a good secret. But that is not usually what happens. Sometimes they talk about something they did or someone they knew. But mostly they just talk.

Sleep comes in **cycles**. There are five parts to a sleep cycle. The first is when you begin to fall asleep. This is called light sleep. In the next part, you are asleep. You do not notice things around you. Then come two

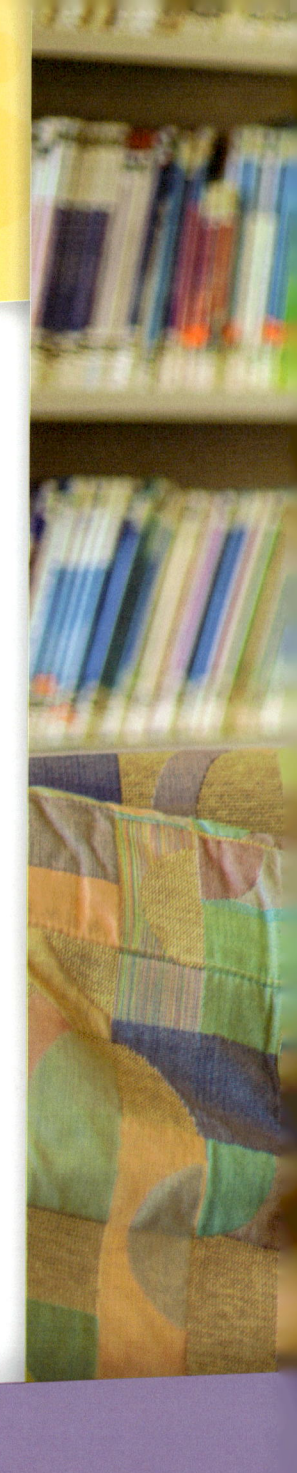

You have probably heard a secret, but it didn't come from someone sleep talking.

9

stages of deep sleep. Your muscles are relaxed. Your body repairs itself. It fixes bones and muscles and fights off disease. Last is **REM** sleep. This is when you dream. The whole cycle lasts about one and a half or two hours. When it ends, a new cycle starts.

Sleep talking can take place any time in the sleep cycle. A person who talks during light sleep is easier to understand. But when he is in deep sleep, it might sound like **gibberish**. Usually, people only talk for about 30 seconds at a time.

Sleep talkers might talk several times during the night.

Keeping Others Awake

The next morning, Penny asked Ann what she was talking about during the night. Ann did not remember saying anything. But she was not surprised. At home, Ann and her sister share a bedroom. Sometimes Ann talks so much that her sister cannot go to sleep.

Ann's mom decided to call Dr. Brown. He said people talk in their sleep when they are **stressed**. Stress can come from not getting enough sleep.

A doctor may be able help if sleep talking is related to stress.

Sleeping in a strange place can cause sleep talking. When people take trips, they sleep in new places. They might sleep in a hotel or at a grandparent's house.

Sometimes the trip is long. They might fall asleep in the car. Moving from the car to a bed can cause sleep talking, too.

Sleeping talking might happen during a camping trip.

15

Dr. Brown gave other reasons. Eating large meals or drinking **caffeine** before bedtime can cause sleeping talking. So can certain medicines. Someone who is sick and has a fever might sleep talk. Someone might start screaming while sleeping. The person is probably having **night terrors**. If this happens often, the person should see a doctor.

MAKE A GUESS!

What if someone screams in her sleep? Should you try to wake her? Ask a parent or teacher to help you look for the answer online or at the library.

Eating a lot before going to sleep can cause sleep talking.

17

Routines Can Help

Dr. Brown asked if Ann was **sleepwalking**, too. People sometimes sleepwalk during deep sleep. They might sit up in bed and look around. They might walk through the house or go outside. Some people even drive in their sleep!

Ann does not sleepwalk. But Dr. Brown had ideas she could try to stop sleep talking. To help Ann sleep better, her parents set a bedtime **routine**. First, Ann puts on her pajamas. Then she brushes her hair and

Doing the same thing at the same time every night can help people sleep better.

her teeth. Then she reads a story. Ann goes to bed at the right time. Then she falls asleep.

Ann did not follow her routine at the sleepover. The girls ate snacks and drank soda. They played games for a long time. Then they watched a movie late at night. They fell asleep on the floor in their sleeping bags.

Ann will start her routine again when she gets home. Penny, Ann, and her sister will all get a good night's sleep!

LOOK!

Look for information about how much sleep children need each night. Do you get enough sleep?

Reading on the sofa could make you sleepy, but you shouldn't sleep there.

Think About It

People need different amounts of sleep depending on their age. Why do you think this is so? Create a chart to record the hours you sleep each night for a week. Ask an adult to do the same. How do the actual amounts of sleep compare?

Can you explain to a friend the five parts of the sleep cycle? Go online or visit the library to find a sleep cycle chart. Does this help?

Write about a time when you couldn't get to sleep. Include a list of things you did to help yourself get to sleep.

Glossary

caffeine (kah-FEEN) a substance found in coffee, tea, and soda that keeps people awake

cycles (SYE-kuhlz) series of events that repeat themselves

gibberish (JIB-er-ish) confused talk that doesn't mean anything

night terrors (NITE TER-erz) fear and screaming while asleep

REM (AHR-EE-EM) dreaming period of sleep known as rapid eye movement

routine (roo-TEEN) a regular way of doing something

sleepwalking (SLEEP-waw-king) walking or other actions done while asleep

somniloquy (som-NILL-uh-kwee) sleep talking

stressed (STRESD) having tension in the body or mind

Find Out More

Books:

Colligan, L. H. *Sleep Disorders*. New York: Marshall Cavendish, 2009.

Scott, Elaine. *All About Sleep from A to Zzzz*. New York: Viking, 2008.

Showers, Paul. *Sleep Is for Everyone*. New York: HarperCollins, 1997.

Web Sites:

KidsHealth—What Sleep Is and Why All Kids Need It
http://kidshealth.org/kid/stay_healthy/body/not_tired.html
Play the "Time for Bed" game and learn about why sleep is important to your brain and your body.

Time for Kids—Sleep Tight!
www.timeforkids.com/news/sleep-tight/54321
Find out why sleep is so important for children and adults.

Index

bedtime routine, 18–20

caffeine, 16

deep sleep, 8–10, 18
dreams, 10

eating, 16

fevers, 16

light sleep, 8, 10

medicine, 16

night terrors, 16

REM sleep, 10

screaming, 16
sickness, 16
sleep cycles, 8–10
sleepovers, 4, 20
sleepwalking, 18
somniloquy, 6
strange places, 14
stress, 12

trips, 14

About the Author

Samantha Bell is a children's writer and illustrator living in South Carolina with her husband, four children, and lots of animals. She has illustrated a number of picture books, including some of her own. She has also written magazine articles, stories, and poems, as well as craft, activity, and wildlife books. She loves animals, being outdoors, and learning about all the amazing wonders of nature.